MY AUSSIE AND THE HIKING BOOTS

Terri Anne Strickland-Odell

WORKBOOK PRESS LLC
187 E Warm Springs Rd,
Suite B285, Las Vegas, NV 89119, USA

Website: https://workbookpress.com/
Hotline: 1-888-818-4856
Email: admin@workbookpress.com

Ordering Information:
Quantity sales. Special discounts are available on quantity purchases by corporations, associations, and others.
For details, contact the publisher at the address above.

ISBN-13:   978-1-957618-82-1 (Paperback Version)
                978-1-957618-83-8 (Digital Version)

REV. DATE: 02/28/2022

Terri Anne Strickland-Odell

Once upon a time, in a beautiful, serene, rural Wyoming town of Buffalo, lived a family of four. This included a young, independent, nature-loving mother named Terrianne, and a young hard working father named Christopher.

Terrianne and Christopher had one child; a beautiful red-headed daughter, named Maryanne. She was quite the adventurous and loved to spend her days outdoors. The fourth member of the family was a little dog. Now, this little dog was an Australian Terrier, named Cookie. Cookie, is such a sweet little dog that she too loves adventures and being outdoors as well.

sniff

One day, Maryanne wanted to spend her day exploring the majestic and melodious mountains of Buffalo with her family.

She sat down with her family and started to plan what she wanted to do and explore.

Maryanne was so excited that she started to think about all the exciting things that they were going to do, and with that, she had trouble trying to sleep. But eventually, she finally did.

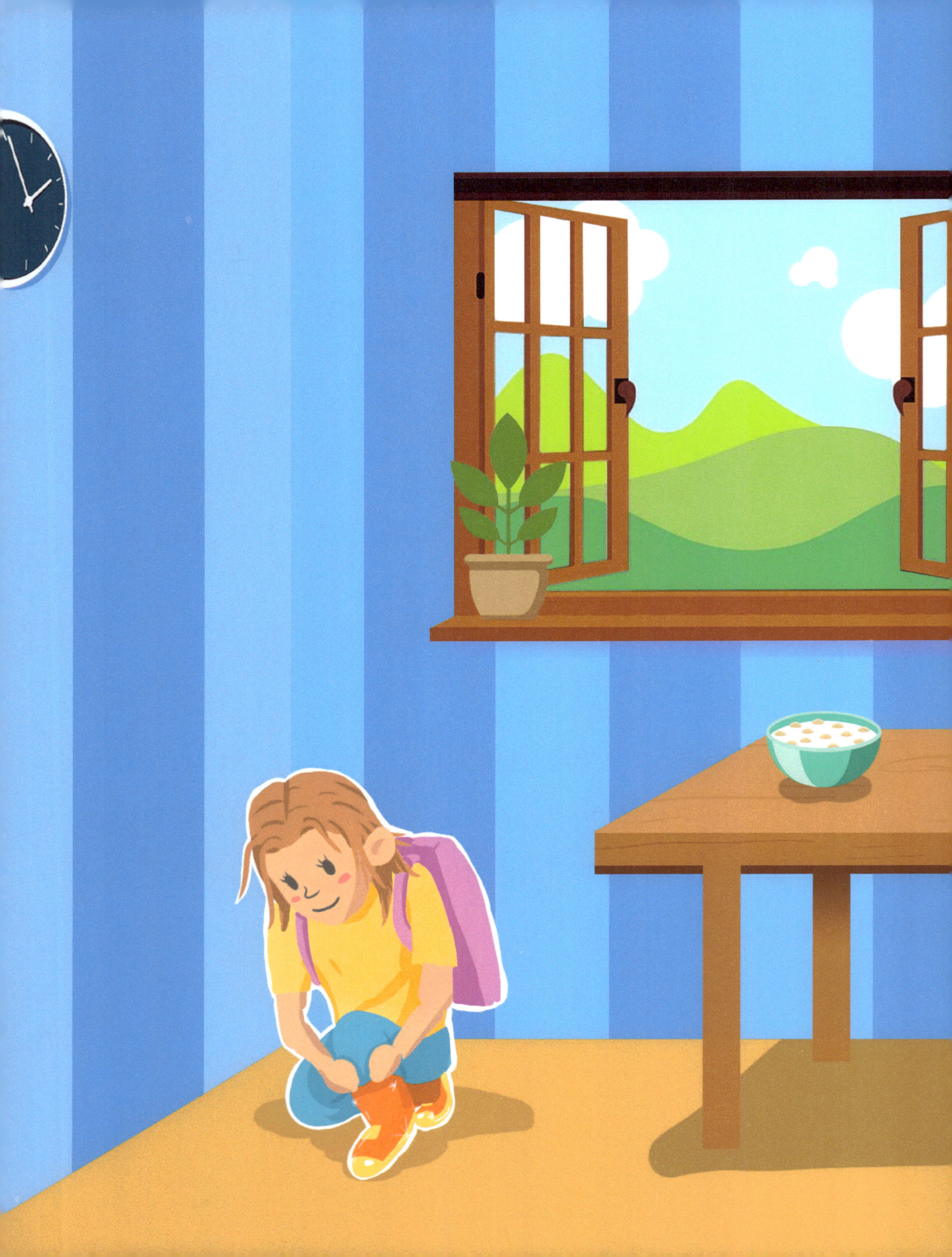

The morning arrived. Maryanne woke up very excited, and so did Cookie. They were ready for their adventure. So then, she got dressed and was ready for her breakfast.

After their breakfast, Maryanne put on her exploring shoes, which were hiking boots. Not just any boots, but exploring hiking boots. These were very special to Maryanne because once she put these boots on, she was an explorer for the mountains.

Once Maryanne was ready and finished breakfast along with Cookie, they were ready to go out and go discover things. Her parents told Maryanne, that they wanted her and Cookie to go out and find a pretty and full Christmas Tree for that Christmas. She must mark it with a special object so they would know how to find it.

Maryanne and Cookie, took their mission very seriously. They then started their adventure in the beautiful Bighorn Mountains. While in the Bighorn's, they found a trail that led to a calm and clear mountain stream.

While they followed the stream, the stream seemed to led these two to a group of trees that seem to just have a tree that looked like the description of what Maryanne's mother told her to find. It was tall and very full and super pretty.

Naturally then, Maryanne was very happy that she and Cookie looked for a particular marker to help them find this tree when the time was right.

Then the perfect answer came to Maryanne. She found a pretty ginormous sparkly pink rock. Maryanne and Cookie dug this rock and put it by this tree.

As the day, started to get somewhat dark, Maryanne was so excited to tell her parents what they found and how they marked it for them to find later on.

Her parents were so happy about their adventure that they could hardly wait to see their discovery.

As the time grew closer, Maryanne and Cookie were ready to show her parents where this tree was and how they marked it. When they got there, her parents saw this beautiful tree and then saw this pink sparkly rock marking it.

COOKIE

Now it's Christmas time, and there is white snow on the ground. The family took this tree to their home and they also took the pink sparkly rock which they share with the tree. As the tree is decorated it seems to be happy and sparkly with the pink rock.

Thank you, God
What new adventure
can we find tomorrow?

It's now bedtime.

    Maryanne and Cookie are in bed saying their prayers. In their prayers, Maryanne says 'Thank You, God for my hiking boots and my Aussie' and another 'Thank You', especially for helping them with their discovery.

    As Maryanne starts to drift asleep, you can hear her say softly, "What new adventure can we find tomorrow?"

The End!

www.ingramcontent.com/pod-product-compliance
Lightning Source LLC
Chambersburg PA
CBHW041923180726
48295CB00002B/64